First published in 1984 by Child's Play (International) Ltd
Ashworth Road, Bridgemead, Swindon SN5 7YD

Published in USA by Child's Play Inc
250 Minot Avenue, Auburn, Maine 04210

Distributed in Australia by Child's Play Australia Pty Ltd
Unit 10/20 Narabang Way
Belrose, NSW 2085

ISBN 978-0-85953-182-5
CLP150519CPL06191825

Printed and bound in Shenzhen, China

This impression 2019/1

Library of Congress Catalogue Number 90-46414
A catalogue record of this book is available from the British Library

www.childs-play.com

The Little Mouse,
the Red Ripe Strawberry, and

THE BIG HUNGRY BEAR

by Don and Audrey Wood · illustrated by Don Wood

Hello, little Mouse.
What are you doing?

Oh, I see.

Are you going to pick
that red, ripe strawberry?

But, little Mouse,
haven't you heard
about the big,
hungry Bear?

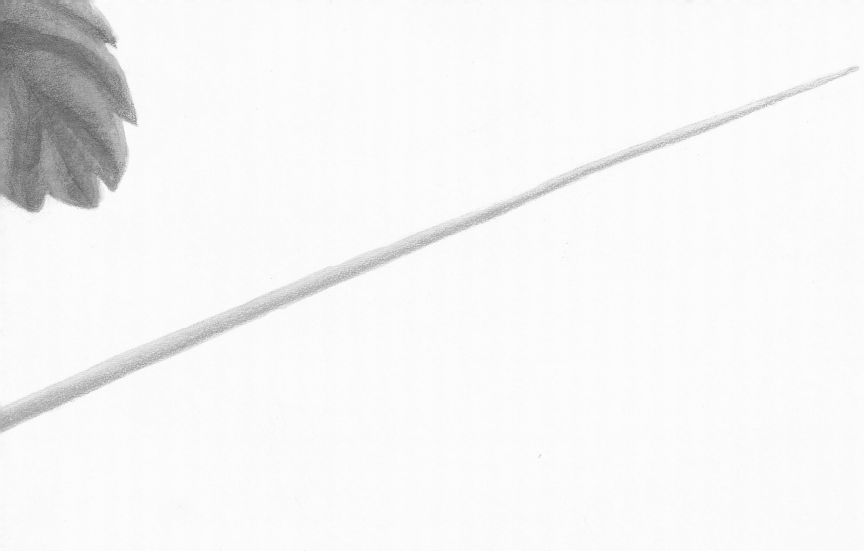

Ohhh, how that Bear
loves red, ripe strawberries!

The big, hungry Bear
can smell a red, ripe
strawberry a mile away...

Especially, one that has
just been picked.

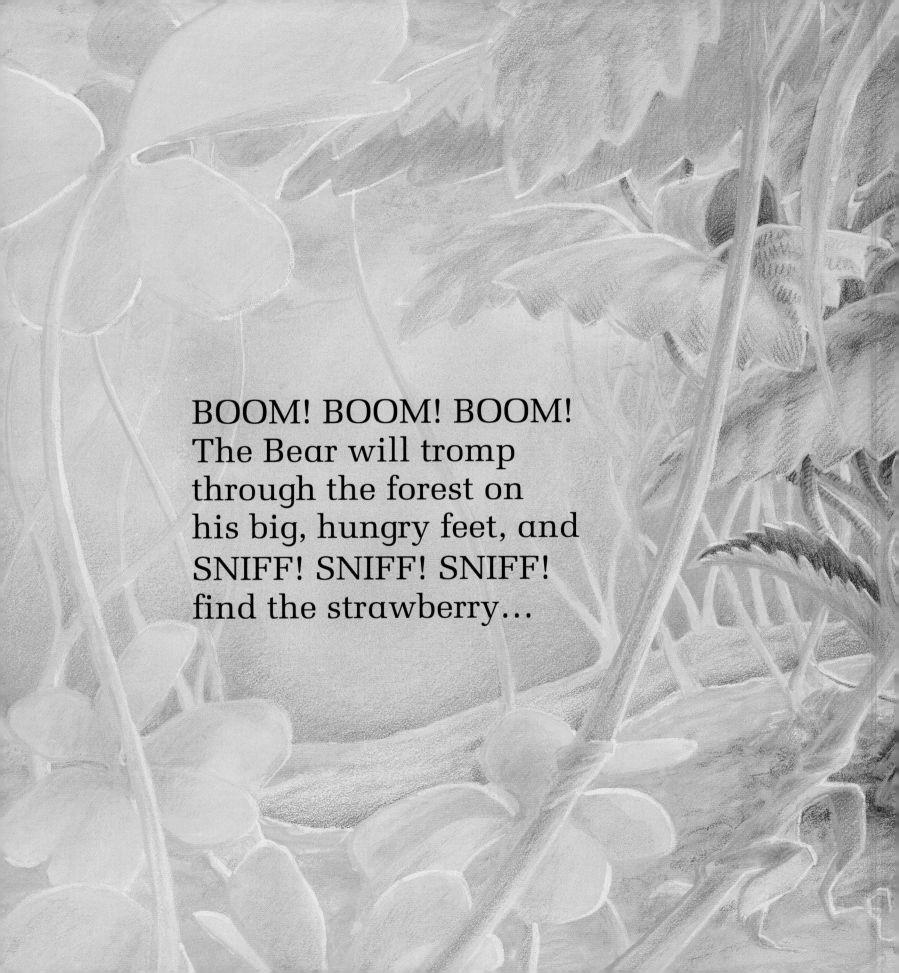

BOOM! BOOM! BOOM!
The Bear will tromp
through the forest on
his big, hungry feet, and
SNIFF! SNIFF! SNIFF!
find the strawberry…

No matter where
it is hidden,

or who is guarding it,

or how it is disguised.

Quick! There's only one way in the whole wide world to save a red, ripe, strawberry from the big, hungry Bear!

Cut it in two.

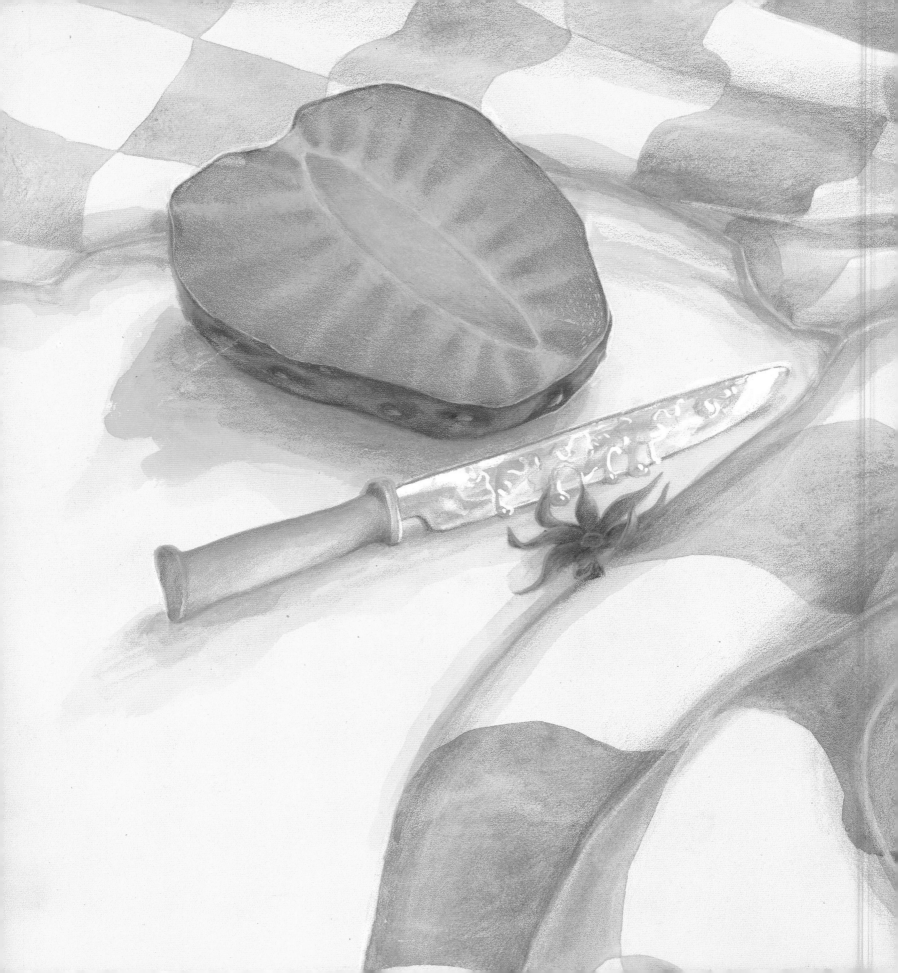

Share half with me.

And we'll both eat it
all up. YUM!

Now, that's one red, ripe
strawberry the big, hungry
Bear will never get!

The End